First published by Parragon in 2007

Parragon
Queen Street House
4 Queen Street
Bath BA1 1HE, UK

ISBN 978-1-4054-9472-4
Printed in China

The Penguin who wanted to sparkle

Illustrated by Sophie Groves   Written by Kath Smith

PaRragon

Bath · New York · Singapore · Hong Kong · Cologne · Delhi · Melbourne

One moonlit night, Mommy penguin's egg went CRACK! A tiny beak appeared, then a head, followed by two tiny wings and a pair of orange feet.

A fluffy little penguin chick called Pip hopped out.
"Pretty sparkles!" she squeaked, as she gazed up at the sparkly stars
in the sky.

Then Pip saw a lot of funny fish jumping out of the ocean waves—SPLASH! They were all shiny and sparkly.

"I want to sparkle, too," squeaked the little penguin excitedly.

Soon it began to snow. Pip watched the snowflakes floating down, sparkling as they fell.

"If I catch some, I can sprinkle them on my feathers," she thought. "Then I will sparkle, too."

Pip ran around, trying to catch the snowflakes. But they just melted on her wings. "Where have the sparkles gone?" she wondered.

Pip found a bank of powdery white snow. It twinkled in the moonlight. "Now I will sparkle!" she cried, rolling over and over in the snowy drift.

But the moon disappeared
behind a cloud. The snow stopped
twinkling, and Pip's feathers
didn't sparkle one tiny bit.

"Maybe I can catch a sparkly star," thought Pip,
jumping up and down. But she couldn't reach one,
however hard she tried. Poor Pip felt very sad.

"What are you doing, Pip?" asked the other penguins.
"Why do you look so sad?"

"I'm trying to catch some sparkles," Pip explained. So they all tried to help. They hopped and they jumped. They rolled and they wriggled. But they couldn't catch any sparkles, however hard they tried.

Just then a friendly whale swam by. "All that jumping and rolling about looks very tiring!" he laughed. "Why don't you come and slide on my back instead?"

Everyone agreed this was a wonderful idea—even Pip.
One by one, the penguins whooshed down the whale's
back and landed in the glittering sea. SPLASH!

Pip hopped out of the water and shook
her wet feathers in the sunshine.
"Look!" cried the other penguins.
"You're sparkling all over!"

Pip danced happily in the snow.
"So THAT'S how you sparkle—
by having fun in the sun. Come on,
everyone. Let's have another go!"